The Unclaimed Christmas Gift

By Alissa Dunn

PublishAmerica
Baltimore

ISBN: 1-4241-4774-3
PUBLISHED BY PUBLISHAMERICA, LLLP
www.publishamerica.com
Baltimore

Printed in the United States of America

This book is dedicated to God, and my family and friends who believe in my work and encourage me to keep writing. I love you all. A special thanks goes out to my mother. Your Christian guidance and encouragement through the years made this book possible.

Foreword

This is a collection of fictional short stories centered on Christmas. The first three stories were written with children in mind, but can be appreciated by adults as well. The last three stories were created with grown-ups in mind, but children may also enjoy. I encourage you to read the stories as a family as you celebrate the Christmas season. All of the stories are Christian-based, and each has a special message for everyone out there.

God bless you, and enjoy the stories!

Floyd's Christmas Wish

Chapter One

The big gust of wind nearly blew Floyd off of his perch atop the tall blade of grass. He clamped down tighter with his hands and feet to hold on. The wind blew harder, which caused him to sway back and forth in the breeze like the needle on a metronome.

No matter how hard the wind blew, Floyd held on tighter. He thought he might just stay up there all night. That is, until he heard his mother calling.

"Floyd!" she hollered, her voice barely audible above the wind, "Get down from there before you get yourself killed! Come down and get in this house right now!"

Floyd sat poised, looking toward the sky, determined to continue practicing until the last possible moment. He couldn't possibly come down—he had to strengthen his body. If he was ever going to make it all the way to the North Pole, he had to be ready to fly.

He tuned out the world around him, all except for himself and the wind. He pictured himself standing very statuesque against the wind's fury—the most noble and brave grasshopper of them all.

"Floyd Hoppermeyer, you'd better get down from there right now before I send your father to get you!" his mother hollered, quite seriously that time.

With a heavy sigh, Floyd carefully backed down the slope of grass until he couldn't see the sky any longer amidst the jungle of the grass blades around him. Once his two back legs touched the soft ground, he turned to his mother. She had that ever-so-familiar motherly look of scorn on her face.

"I'm sorry, Ma. I was practicing for my trip and I didn't hear you," he fibbed.

"Save your story for when your father gets home. I am sick and tired of telling you the same thing over and over, and you won't listen. You know, one day you are going to get yourself in a real mess, and I won't be here to get you out of trouble," his mother scolded.

Suddenly, a thunderous sound enveloped them, and the grass began to sway around fiercely. Floyd's father swooped in, stirring up dust with his powerful wings.

"Did I hear someone talking about me?" he asked.

"Yes. You need to do something with that boy of

yours. He's been up the grass blade again, thinking of those ridiculous ideas. He won't listen to me. It's time you did something about it, Harvey," Mrs. Hoppermeyer said.

Harvey trod over to his wife and gently smoothed her delicate wings with his two right arms. He always knew how to calm her down when she was in a tizzy.

"After dinner, sweetheart. I had a bad day. I almost got chopped up by a lawn mower today. Those things will take your head clean off! I got sucked right in before I knew what had me! I was whirling around in there for about an hour, flying against the wind!

"I almost got pulled into the cutting blade a couple of times, but I decided to say my prayers and head for the grass chute! I dodged the blade and flew right out the side. I spent the next few minutes escaping the gigantic teeth of a huge cat, a toddler who wanted to stick me to his lollipop, and a lizard that thought I would make a nice side dish to her spider casserole! I tell ya', it's enough to starve a guy. Let's eat!"

The parents turned and looked at Floyd, whose eyes bulged out in shock at what he had just heard. Darla burst out laughing, and Harvey joined right in.

"Oh, Harvey, you are such a cut-up—no pun intended," she giggled.

Floyd exhaled with relief. His father was notorious for being a jokester, but he was also the strongest, smartest, and fastest grasshopper around. It wasn't unreasonable to think his story could have been true.

Darla took the lid off of her hollowed-out acorn, revealing the milkweed stew she had made for their supper. She dished it out, and it didn't take long before they had slurped it all down.

Floyd helped clear the dishes from the table before going to his room. He lay back on the bed of soft leaves and looked up at the ceiling of grass. Would he ever get to the North Pole? It sounded like such a wonderful place.

Floyd's home was right under one of the windows of the humans' house. The humans had a magical box that was called a television. When they turned it on, he sometimes heard stories about the North Pole.

Floyd had learned all about the North Pole from the humans. The people of the North Pole, called "elves," were quite jolly and fun. That Santa character and his reindeer were certainly very nice, and they all worked together to make Christmas special for everyone. There was a workshop where they built toys, baked lots and lots of cookies, and wrapped presents—all year 'round. Floyd didn't know what cookies were, but they sounded like something good.

Floyd was interrupted from his thoughts when his father poked his head into the room.

"Son, are you asleep?" his father asked.

"No, Pop," Floyd answered.

Harvey entered the room and came over to sit beside the bed.

"What's this your mother tells me about you wanting to go to the North Pole?" Harvey asked.

Floyd hesitated, fearful that he would be laughed at for sharing his feelings. He began slowly telling the details of his dream to travel to the North Pole.

His father listened patiently and intently, so Floyd continued sharing his plans in a little more detail. Then, he waited for his father's rebuttal.

"Son, the North Pole is a mighty long way from here, and it's cold up there—very cold," Harvey began. He saw the look of disappointment begin to creep into Floyd's tiny, green face. He couldn't bear to hurt his child's feelings.

"But, if you work really hard, and you have a positive attitude, you can do just about anything," he continued.

Floyd perked right up. At least his father was listening to him.

"It never hurts to have a dream, Floyd, just as long as you don't forget to pay attention to what is going on right now. That means you can dream about going to the North Pole some day, but if your mother tells you to do something now, you had better listen to her. Do you understand, Son?" Harvey asked.

"Yes, Sir. Thank you, Pop!" Floyd answered.

"Just doing my job as a dad. Good night, sleep tight, and remember to eat the bed bugs before they bite," Hal said. He tucked Floyd in and went to get into his own bed.

Floyd felt better after the talk with his father, but he still wouldn't give up. His dream was not to go to the North Pole some day—it was to get to the North Pole by this Christmas—or else!

As he lay awake in his bed, he heard the humans shuffling out onto their back patio. It sounded like the father and the young one.

"See that star, Son?" the father asked. "You should make a wish on it. Some people say that if you make a wish on the first star you see at night, your wish will come true."

Floyd couldn't believe his ears. Could it be that easy? He knew exactly what to wish for. He jumped off of his bed and climbed just high enough through the grass to see the sky. When the bright, glittery light of a star shone through the peep hole, he made his wish to see the North Pole. He sure hoped it worked.

Chapter Two

The next several weeks went by very quickly for Floyd. He spent most of his afternoons practicing his flying and long distance hopping. His legs were quite sore at first, but it didn't take long for his muscles to get used to the extra work.

He began his training by jumping around the outside of his house, and then he moved on to hopping from grass blade to grass blade, until he could skip over a couple in the middle.

One afternoon, Floyd decided it would be good practice to try and jump over the shrubs next to the humans' house. He carefully climbed up a tall blade of grass to scope out the territory. He made sure there were no cats or lizards lurking around looking for their dinner. The coast was clear. The children were inside their home, so he didn't have to worry about them. This was the perfect time!

He leapt from one blade of grass to another, until he landed right under the base of a large, green shrub. It looked pretty high from where Floyd sat. It was a little bigger than the humans' toddler, as his father called the creature. If he was going to go out into the world, he had to be able to jump over things like that shrub.

Floyd took a deep breath, then hopped and flapped his little wings with all his might—which landed him smack dab in the middle of the shrub, making him come face to face with a big, fat spider!

Floyd screamed. The spider's eyes widened in fear, and she screamed, too!

"You get out of my house, you little peeping Tom! How dare you try to come in here and peek at me when I ain't got nothin' on?" she exclaimed. She gave him a shove with two of her legs while covering her private parts with two more.

Floyd went hurtling out of the bush and landed on the ground with a thump. Once he shook off the jolt, he looked back up to the spot from which he had been so brutally accosted. That was a close call, indeed. He wanted nothing more than to run back home crying to his mother, but he remembered what his father had told him about working hard.

He got back up on his feet, took a few steps back, and

got a running start. He took a huge leap this time. He flew higher and higher, up past the spider lady. She saw him fly by and screamed again. He managed to make it over the top of the bush and down to the other side.

"Ahh ha ha!" Floyd hollered out with joy. He jumped back over to the other side, alarming the spider lady again. He leapt over the bush about three more times, and each time Floyd jumped, the spider lady screamed and covered herself.

On the last jump, he saw that the she had fainted from all the excitement. It was probably best for him to get out of there before she woke up and decided to eat him after all.

Floyd's success with the shrubs made him even more adventurous. Soon after, he was leaping over lawn furniture, the humans' grill, the neighbor's old hound dog named Pete, and anything else taller than himself. He knew he was finally ready.

Christmas would be coming very soon. The snow hadn't come yet, but the temperature had dropped until it was downright cold. Floyd's mother wouldn't let him go outside very much, so he had to practice in his room when he couldn't go out.

One cold winter evening, Floyd lay awake in his bed, listening to the humans' television. He heard all about some guy named Frosty, some fellow named Rudolph, and a few other characters.

He had almost drifted off to sleep when he heard the most beautiful sound of all. It was singing. The big people, most likely the mom and dad, were singing near their window.

"You better watch out, you better not cry, you better not pout, I'm telling you why. Santa Claus is coming to town."

Wow! It was true! Santa was on his way! He had to act fast! Maybe if he caught Santa on his way through town, he could follow him to the North Pole!

Floyd quietly got up from his bed and left his room, peeking around every corner throughout the house to make sure he didn't wake his parents.

Once Floyd was out of his home, he walked a little way through the grass so his parents would not hear his powerful takeoff. When he was certain that he was out of earshot of his parents, he shimmied up a blade of grass to see where he was.

It was quite cold out, and the wind was howling wildly. Floyd was more than ready to tough it out, though. He had to make it to the roof atop the humans' house. That's where Santa would make his landing.

Floyd leapt as high and as far as he could, just as he had practiced. He leapt for what felt like miles until he reached the gutter, which ran up the corner of the house and to the roof. He jumped onto the side of the gutter, his feet clinking against the metal. Once he had a firm grip, he slowly began climbing.

The wind had grown fiercer, the air icier. Little droplets of moisture began to fall from the sky, attaching to the gutter and to Floyd's body. He flapped his wings to dry himself off.

Soon, the water turned to snow as big flakes drifted down from the sky, adhering to the shrubs and grass below.

Floyd paused to track his progress. He was more than halfway up the gutter. The snow was coming down so hard that he couldn't even see the tree line anymore, but he kept moving.

By the time Floyd finally reached the top of the gutter, it had grown very slick from the accumulation of ice. He couldn't possibly hold on there much longer, but he only had about six inches left to go.

His feet began to lose their grip on the gutter as the ice continued forming. He tried to regain traction, but slipped even more. It was such a long way down if he took a fall. He flapped his stiff little wings as hard as he could.

The wind gusted harder, nearly blowing him out into the wilderness, but Floyd kept beating his wings until they carried him to the rooftop. It had become so cold that Floyd's little body shivered and shook in the freezing air. He anchored his feet to the shingles, hoping that Santa would come soon.

The snow storm had begun to calm, but not soon

enough for Floyd. He was not used to being outside during this kind of weather. He needed to move around to keep warm, but he was afraid to let go of the shingles. He knew he would be blown right off of the roof if he let go. He tried moving one leg at a time while holding on with the others, but it didn't help to warm him up any.

Floyd began to feel very tired. He tried to hold on to the roof, but couldn't do it any longer. His little legs gave out, and he collapsed onto the roof in the icy slush. He tried to flap his wings, but they were frozen. All he wanted to do was sleep, just sleep now. His eyes closed, even as he tried to force them to stay open. His only thought was that he was not going to make it to the North Pole.

Chapter Three

"Is he all right?" the reindeer with the little red nose asked. He lit up his nose a little brighter so everyone could see Floyd lying in the snow.

"It's hard to tell for certain," Santa replied as he picked up Floyd's tiny green body from the rooftop where he stood.

"It's a good thing you spotted him, Rudie," another reindeer said.

Santa placed Floyd on the front seat of his sled, where he kept a blanket for warmth. He tucked Floyd in, and then went to the backseat where he kept a first aid kit for emergencies such as these. He pulled out a thermos filled with Mrs. Claus' home made hot cocoa. He removed the cap, stuck his finger in to get a bit of the cocoa, and gently touched the sweet, warm liquid to Floyd's lips. Floyd did not drink, nor did he move.

"Is he going to make it, Santa?" Rudie asked.

"I'm afraid that isn't up to me. What we need is a miracle. You know those only come from one place. Let's call upon the founder of Christmas, God himself," Santa replied.

Santa knelt in the snow on the roof top of the humans' house, and folded his hands together as he propped them on the sled in front of Floyd's little body.

"Dear Heavenly Father," Santa began as he bowed his head, and the reindeer also bowed theirs, "We give thanks to You for this season, as it reminds us of Your ultimate sacrifice for us. We thank You for the gift of Jesus, and what he means to all of us. A miracle happened over two thousand years ago with the birth of Your son, Jesus.

"As we celebrate that miracle tonight, delivering gifts to children the world over, I would like to ask for just one more miracle, if it is Your will. Please help this little grasshopper. I know he was waiting for me. One of my elves told me about it right before I left, but I thought it might have been a mistake. I will leave him in Your hands, and thank You in advance for Your wonderful mercy and grace, in the name of Jesus, Amen."

Santa arose from his position and wiped his eyes. He always teared up when he talked to the Lord. He turned his attention back to Floyd, who had remained in the same position. Santa took one more dab of hot cocoa and applied it to Floyd's lips.

A moment later, the green color began to creep its way back into Floyd's face. His little lips parted, and his tongue savored the cocoa. His eyes fluttered open, just so slightly at first, until they finally popped open. When they focused on the man in the red suit, his eyes grew even wider with amazement.

"It's a miracle! You sure had us worried, youngster!" the man said, as he picked Floyd up so gently in the palm of his hand.

"Are you Santa? Is this the North Pole?" Floyd asked.

"Well, I am Santa, but this sure isn't the North Pole! It's too warm here to be the North Pole. We found you on the roof where you collapsed. We thought you were a goner, until the good Lord answered our prayers for you. Now what in the world are you doing up here on this roof?"

Floyd explained his dream of going to the North Pole and how he thought he could catch a ride when Santa came through. He never realized that his little bug body wouldn't last in the cold.

"I guess I can't come with you now," Floyd told Santa, his little shoulders drooping.

"No, Floyd. I am afraid you can't come to the North Pole. But, I'll tell you what I can do. I'll bring a little of the North Pole to you," Santa said. He sat Floyd back down on the seat of the sleigh and then reached deep into his big red bag of goodies.

Santa pulled out a box of Mrs. Claus' hot cocoa mix,

and a large snow globe with scenery inside it of the North Pole. He placed them both beside Floyd on the front seat of the sleigh and waved his hand over them. Both items shrunk to be just Floyd's size.

Santa reached in his pocket and pulled out a tiny little red coat, just like his own — only much, much smaller. He helped Floyd to put it on his little body, and then he produced a tiny red hat for Floyd's head.

"Floyd, I think you are all set for Christmas now. What do you say we get you back home?" Santa asked.

"Oh, thank you Santa! Thank you!" Floyd exclaimed.

Santa snapped his fingers. Floyd opened his eyes and found himself back in his own bed. It was daylight outside. Floyd was so disappointed. He surely had been dreaming.

A moment later, his mother came into his room to wake him up for Christmas breakfast. "Floyd, dear, it's time to get up. Merry Christmas!"

Suddenly, her facial expression changed to a slight frown and she cocked her head to one side. She stepped closer to get a better look at Floyd. "Oh my! What's that you are wearing?"

Floyd looked down to see the little red coat still on his body. He looked around and saw his hat on the floor beside his bed, along with the snow globe and hot cocoa tin.

"I guess Santa came to see me, Mama," Floyd

answered. Maybe after Christmas he would tell the whole story.

"Let's share my cocoa, Mama," Floyd said, as he brought the tin into the kitchen.

The Hoppermeyer family sat around the kitchen table, sharing hot cocoa and listening to the humans opening their gifts and singing Christmas carols.

Floyd Hoppermeyer wouldn't trade this moment for any he could find at the North Pole. Home was right where he wanted to be.

A Christmas Hero

Chapter One

Malcolm Johnson wanted, more than anything else in the whole world, a Sergeant Dave Deputy-On-Patrol action figure, complete with a super-charged police cruiser with working blue lights and siren. He carefully circled the items in the brand new Super Mart color catalog. Back in August, Malcolm had asked for the toy for his birthday, but he received a new winter coat instead. His father had lost his job at the tire factory, so money was very tight.

"I know it isn't what you wanted, Malcolm. You can't play with it, and it isn't even that fashionable, but you'll need it for winter," his mother had said.

"I know, Mama, but it's August, and it is too hot for a coat. Why can't I have a toy?" Malcolm had asked.

"We couldn't afford it, Malcolm. I bought the coat several months ago and put it back in the closet for this winter, but I wanted you to have something for your birthday, and that is all I could give you. I know you don't understand, but I'm doing the best I can. Maybe you will get a Deputy Dave doll for Christmas," she answered.

"Mom! It's *Sergeant* Dave, not Deputy Dave, and it isn't a doll. It's an *action figure*. Dolls are for girls!" Malcolm retorted.

"Well, it doesn't matter *what* he is, you aren't getting the toy until I say so!" she scolded.

Malcolm had spent the rest of the day in his room, and he was placed on television restriction for a whole week for having a smart mouth.

Ever since that day, he worked very hard at behaving. His mother worked a part-time job on most evenings, so Malcolm helped out by washing dishes every night. He swept the kitchen floor, and he cleaned his room, too. He even offered to mow the grass, but his mother refused since he was only nine years old. She was afraid he would cut his feet instead of the lawn.

Malcolm's father came home one afternoon with great news.

"I've got a job! It doesn't pay as much as I made at the old plant, but at least we'll have another paycheck coming in again," he said.

"Where is it?" Malcolm asked.

"I'll be working at the service station down the street doing oil changes on cars. Maybe when an opening comes up for a service manager or lead mechanic, I can apply for that position, but this one will have to do for now. That's not such a bad thing," he shrugged.

"I am happy that you got a job, Dad!" Malcolm smiled.

"Me, too, Mal. Don't get too excited just yet. We'll still be tight on money for a little while, so we'll just have to make do with what we have," he said.

The television screen flipped from the evening news to a commercial. It was Sergeant Dave! Malcolm sang along to all the words.

Look out, crooks — it's Sergeant Dave!
He's gonna put an end to your crime wave
He puts crooks in jail where they belong
Grab your deputy badge and come along!
You'll be cruising the streets, looking for thugs
And telling little kids to say no to drugs!
You'll be a big hero for being so brave,
and riding along with Sergeant Dave!

Sergeant Dave action figure comes complete with handcuffs, badge and hat. Cruiser, uniform accessory pack, and crooks sold separately.

Attention, kids! Sergeant Dave is coming to your town!

He'll be making a very special appearance at the Super Mart on East Ridge Drive on December 24th. Yes, that's Christmas Eve! While your mom and dad are doing their last minute shopping for Christmas cookies to leave for Santa, you can visit the real Sergeant Dave! He'll be there from 4 to 7 P.M., so be there on time for your chance to shake the hand of a hero!

"Mom! Dad! Did you hear that? Did you? Sergeant Dave is going to be at Super Mart on Christmas Eve. Can we go?" Malcolm asked.

"I don't know. I think I have to work," his mother answered, shaking her head.

"Dad? What about you? Please, please, pretty please?" Malcolm was hopping up and down with every word.

"I've got to work until six o'clock, but I should be able to pick you up from your sitter and get you over there in time if we hurry," his father answered.

"Yes!" Malcolm pumped his fisted arms in the air and danced around the living room. He was going to see the real Sergeant Dave, live and in person!

Malcolm made a strong effort to be on his best behavior for the next several weeks. He didn't want to mess up his only chance at meeting Sergeant Dave.

On the afternoon of December 24th, Malcolm waited patiently at Mrs. Pettigrew's house for his father to come and pick him up after work. Malcolm paced the floors with excitement. His stomach rolled with anticipation. He was too excited to even eat his afternoon snack of cookies and milk.

"Malcolm, would you please have a seat? You are beginning to make me nervous, pacing around all over the floor like that. Besides, if you keep that up, I'm going to have bald places on my carpet for sure!" Mrs. Pettigrew said.

"I'm sorry. It's just that we're supposed to go see Sergeant Dave today at Super Mart, and I don't want to be late," Malcolm answered.

"I see. I knew it had to be something awfully important for you to turn down my triple-chocolate-caramel-butter-fudge-walnut-praline-sugar cookies. You have never turned down a cookie in all the years I have been keeping you," she said. She giggled, causing her plump middle to jiggle. "Now, how about settling down for a few minutes before you drive me crazy?"

"Yes, ma'am," Malcolm answered as he plopped down on the couch.

It was too hard for him to keep still, though. He clasped his hands to keep them from twitching, but his foot started tapping, then his leg began bouncing up and down. Thump! Thump! Thump!

"Mrs. Pettigrew, what time is it?" he asked.

"It's only a few minutes after the last time you asked. It is six-thirty," she answered.

"Where is my dad? He's late! We're going to miss Sergeant Dave!" Malcolm cried.

His father pulled into the driveway of Mrs. Pettigrew's house at six forty-five.

Malcolm ran outside and hopped into the car before his father had a chance to shut it off and come inside.

Mrs. Pettigrew waved goodbye from the doorway.

"Floor it, Dad! We've got to get to Super Mart fast!" Malcolm said as he buckled his seatbelt.

"Well, hello to you, too, Son!" his father smirked as he put the car into reverse and backed out of the driveway.

Malcolm thought his father could have driven much faster than they were traveling, but he knew better than to ask his father to speed up. Instead, he silently prayed for a chance to meet Sergeant Dave.

When they arrived at Super Mart, the line of people who were waiting to see Sergeant Dave was quite long. The big electric sliding doors of the store were propped open, and the light from inside shone out onto the dark parking lot. The light illuminated the snake-like line of people that wrapped all the way from the front door, around the side of the building, and back to the rear garden entrance of the store.

Malcolm's father dropped him off at the end of the line and told him to stay right there and not to move while he went and parked the car. His father finally found a spot at the very rear of the parking lot, and it took him a while to walk back to the place where Malcolm was standing in line.

The temperature outside was quite cold, and the children were all shivering. Some were puffing out air from their mouths so they could see their own breath. A few kids were crying that they had to go to the bathroom. One of the mothers said to her daughter, "Just hold it. If we go to the bathroom now, we'll lose our place in line."

Malcolm decided he could hold it until he popped. He wasn't giving up his place in line for anything.

After about twenty minutes, a woman wearing a Super Mart uniform came out to the crowd. She was carrying a megaphone.

"Attention, please!" she shouted through the loud speaker, "I am sorry, folks, but Sergeant Dave has to get back on patrol. I know you have waited a long time to see him, but he must leave. He will not be seeing anymore kids tonight. Sergeant Dave wishes he could see all of you, but for those who didn't get to meet him, we have a special coupon for your parents for ten percent off of the purchase of a Sergeant Dave action figure. Thanks for coming folks," the lady blurted from the megaphone. She turned and walked away quickly to avoid the angry parents and children.

Many of the parents followed her into the store, their children screaming and crying. Malcolm's father went into the store as well, instructing Malcolm to stay put again. There were still plenty of parents and kids standing around near him.

A girl, who appeared to be about eleven years old, was sitting on one of the swings that was on display near where Malcolm was standing.

"You know, it won't do any good to complain. Once he has to leave, he can't help it. He has to go to work. He won't come back out," the little girl said to Malcolm.

"How do you know?" Malcolm asked.

"Haven't you ever been to one of these things before?" she asked.

"No," Malcolm answered, slightly embarrassed to admit that to the girl.

"Well, I have. I've been to tons of these. This sort of thing happens all the time. I'm waiting for my dad to come out so we can go home. It's freezing out here," the girl said as she shivered in her seat.

"Why aren't you wearing a coat?" Malcolm asked.

"My mom's in the hospital. She's really sick. She won't be home for Christmas. I went to visit her today, and I left my coat there by accident. My dad's working here part-time to help pay the bills," she answered.

"They won't let you wait inside?" he asked.

"I was in there for a while, but they said that it was too crowded with all the other kids, and that I was in the way. The store manager made me come out here," she answered.

Malcolm's father came back to the line, and he didn't look happy. "Mal, I am sorry. Sergeant Dave had to go. Maybe we'll catch him another day. I'll go get the car and pick you up, okay?"

"Okay, Dad," Malcolm sighed. He was so disappointed that he wanted to cry, but he didn't want anyone to see him cry, especially a girl. He turned his gaze back to the shivering little girl. She wore a thin turtle neck sweater and a pair of corduroy pants.

"So, what do you think you're going to get for Christmas tomorrow?" Malcolm asked her, thinking it would make them both feel better to talk about something else.

"I don't think I'm getting anything. My parents are really low on money, and I just want my mom to get well. If I can get that for Christmas, then I'll be happy. I just want us all to be home together," she answered.

Malcolm began to feel ashamed of himself. All this time, he had been so obsessed with a toy that he couldn't think about anything else, and the only thing this girl wanted was to be at home with her mother.

As his father pulled up to the curb, Malcolm pulled off his coat and handed it to the girl.

"I know it isn't a girlie coat, but it will keep you warm. I hope your mom gets better soon," Malcolm said.

"Thanks," she said as she put it on.

"Malcolm! What are you doing? That is your new coat!

Why did you give it to her?" his father asked as Malcolm entered the car and closed the door behind him.

"Dad, I know. Please don't be mad. Her mama is sick, and she won't be home for Christmas. Her dad is inside working, and she was cold. I can still wear last year's coat, even with the holes. Please don't make me take it back from her," Malcolm said.

His father sighed, and then leaned forward to get a better look at the lonely little girl on the swing. "Okay. We'll see what we can do about getting a new coat for you after Christmas," he said.

Chapter Two

On Christmas morning, Malcolm woke up to the smell of bacon and eggs being fried on the stove. He followed the smell to the kitchen, where his mother was making breakfast.

"Merry Christmas, Malcolm! Have a seat, and I'll fix you a plate. We'll go into the living room after we eat."

They enjoyed their crispy bacon and fried eggs with toast. Malcolm had a tall glass of milk while his parents drank coffee.

Once the table was cleared, they went into the living room. Malcolm spotted two presents under the tree, both with his name on them. While Malcolm's father got a fire started in the fireplace, his mother sat on the couch and pulled out her Bible. This was the routine every year.

Malcolm knew not to touch the presents until she was finished.

Malcolm and his father listened attentively as she read the story of the birth of Jesus from the New Testament of the Bible. When she was finished reading, she closed the Bible and carefully put it away.

"Malcolm, I hope you learned something from the Bible today about Christmas. First of all, Christmas is not just about presents. It's about love. We have an abundance of that in our house, but there are plenty of other children who don't. You should always be thankful that you have a loving family, even if we never have anything else.

"Jesus and his family had to do without a lot of things, too. He was born in a manger—that's a lot like a barn. He had to sleep where animals were kept, but the important thing was that they made it through, and they went on to greater things. Do you understand?"

Malcolm did understand, and he wondered if it was just because he was older now, or if he understood because of what he and his family had been through this year. "Yes, Mama. I get it. Jesus's family had struggles, too," he answered.

"I'm glad you understand. Let's pray, and then you can open your presents," she said.

They bowed their heads as she prayed aloud, "Our Heavenly Father, we want to thank You for what this day means to us. We thank You for giving us the birth of Your son, Jesus, and for what he means in our lives. We thank You for our home and our health. We are thankful that we can all be together and celebrate the gift of life today with each other. We also pray for those who cannot be together, and ask that You bless them today, in the name of Jesus, Amen."

Malcolm's father got up and retrieved the presents from under the tree. He placed them in front of Malcolm before sitting back down on the sofa.

"Open the green one first," his mother said.

Malcolm opened the big green package. He lifted the lid on the box to find a new coat. He tried it on, and it fit perfectly. He was truly glad to have it.

"I heard about you giving your coat to that little girl, Malcolm. I got a small Christmas bonus last night at work, so I stopped and picked up a new jacket for you on the way home. It isn't as nice as the other one, but it will keep you warm," his mother said.

"I like it just fine. Thanks, Mom," Malcolm said.

The next package was wrapped in red paper with green trees on it. He tore open the wrapping to reveal the gift he had so anxiously awaited. It was a Sergeant Dave action figure complete with a cruiser and uniform accessory pack, and it even had batteries with it! Oh, joy! How wonderful it felt to finally hold it in his hands.

A knock came at the door. Malcolm's mother hurried

back to the bedroom since she wasn't wearing any makeup. His father answered the door. It was a policeman.

"Is this the Johnson residence?" the officer asked.

"Yes, it is. Is there a problem, officer?" Malcolm's father asked. He stepped outside and shut the door to speak to the policeman.

Malcolm went to the bedroom to get his mother.

"Mr. Johnson, there is no problem," the officer said, "I just came by to return this coat. My wife is very sick and she is in the hospital. We had to rush over from the hospital to Super Mart last night. I work days on the police force, but I have a second job dressing up as Sergeant Dave. In the rush, my daughter left her coat at the hospital. I believe your son gave his coat to her, and I really appreciate that. I saw the name and address written on the tag and I wanted to return it. Do you mind if I speak to your son?" the man asked.

Malcolm's father brought the officer inside and asked Malcolm to come back into the living room.

"Hello, Malcolm. My name's Sergeant Dave. It's really nice to meet a hero like you," he said as he stuck his hand out to shake Malcolm's.

"Me? A hero?" Malcolm asked.

"Yes! I heard about you giving your coat to a girl who didn't have one last night. That was exactly what a real hero would do. The girl asked me to return the coat to you, and I also have something very special for you," the officer said as he reached into his pocket. He pulled out a shiny silver badge. It was plastic, but it was just as nice as the metal one he wore on his chest.

The officer bent down and pinned the badge on Malcolm's pajama shirt. "Good job, Deputy! Keep up the good work!"

"Sergeant Dave, would you like to stay and have some coffee?" Malcolm's mother asked.

"I'd love to ma'am, but I've got to visit someone in the hospital. It's been really nice meeting you," he said as he made his way to the door.

"Remember Malcolm, it only takes a heart to be a hero. I think you've got it. Don't forget!"

"Yes, Sir! I'll remember. Thanks, Sergeant Dave!" Malcolm said.

They waved goodbye as the officer backed up his patrol car and drove away.

"Wow, Malcolm! That was some great Christmas, huh? You got your favorite toy, and you got to meet the real Sergeant Dave. How does that feel?" his father asked.

"That was awesome, Dad! I'm so glad I got the toy, but I think I like the real Sergeant Dave even better! Most of all, I love being with my family. I love you, Mom and Dad." Malcolm said.

"We love you, too," his parents answered in unison.

"And I love you too, God," Malcolm said as he looked upward.

"I love you," God whispered to the world.

This story is dedicated in memory of the author's father, Lt. David Alley—a former deputy sheriff and a real hero. He was a beloved father, husband, and grandfather who also loved God. He served God through his work and touched the lives of many people, young and old. May God bless the many officers, firefighters, and military employees who faithfully protect us every day. Thank you for your service and personal sacrifices.

An Undersea Christmas

Chapter One

Larry Lobsterman fiddled with the seaweed until he couldn't stand it anymore.

"This is too hard, Dad. I can't make this look right," he said.

"It takes practice, Son. Keep trying. You want to braid it, then string it up along our coral wall like so," Mr. Lobsterman said, showing Larry how to work the strands and braid them into a string.

"Dad, isn't Christmas for humans? Why are *we* decorating our house for Christmas?" Larry asked.

"Believe me, Larry, I know it sounds strange for a family of lobsters to be celebrating a human holiday, but we have a very good reason," Mr. Lobsterman answered.

"Well, what is it?" Larry asked.

"I'll tell you the story later, Son. Now, just keep braiding that seaweed. We have a lot of work to do," he answered.

Larry worked and worked with the seaweed until he finally had the knack of braiding it. He wove the thin, dark-green strands into a braid, and kept going until he had a very long piece of string.

His father took the string and ran it along the top of the outside wall on the front of their coral house. Then, he handed Larry a paint brush and instructed him to paint some empty oyster shells with glow-in-the-dark plankton.

Larry dipped the brush into the big jar of plankton and painted the shells. When he was finished, the shells shone quite brightly. He handed them to his father, who hung them on the string of seaweed.

"There. That should do it. It looks great, doesn't it?" Mr. Lobsterman asked.

"Oh, my goodness! That is just beautiful!" Mrs. Lobsterman exclaimed.

"Thanks, honey. Larry did most of it," Mr. Lobsterman said to his wife.

Mr. Crabclaw, the Lobstermans' neighbor, dropped in to see what was going on.

"What's with all the lights, Hal?" Mr. Crabclaw asked. He had to turn his body sideways to fit through the opening of the Lobstermans' house. "I bet I could see those bright lights all the way from the tropical waters!"

"You know we do this every year, Herb. This year is no different. Are the lights bothering you?" Mr. Lobsterman asked.

"Nope. I thought maybe you were having a party or something. You know me—if there's free food, I'm there! Hey, don't you remember when you did this last year and old Bart Fishmonger from down the street got all bent out of shape over the bright lights? Well, you just better be careful, because he is the president of the homeowners' association this year. He's liable to cause a ruckus about it," Herb warned.

"Well, Herb, if Bart Fishmonger wants to put up a stink about my lights, then he is more than welcome to come by and talk to me about it, shellfish to blowfish. I don't mean anyone any harm by it, and the lights only come on until the little plankton get tired and go to sleep. Besides, it's just for a few days," Mr. Lobsterman said.

Herb, always a hungry crab, had already tuned out Hal and was rummaging through their pantry in search of food.

"You got any monkfish in here? I am starving! My stomach is about to eat itself! Can you hear it rumbling?" Herb asked.

"Herb, we don't have any monkfish. Now you get on back to your own house and have dinner before you eat us out of house and home!" Mrs. Lobsterman said, as she shooed him off.

"Hey! What do you think I am…a hermit crab? I'm just a regular crab, thank you, and that is no way to treat a starving friend!" Herb said with a huff. He spun around and scurried through the opening of the house, kicking up sand all along the floor.

Mrs. Lobsterman turned bright red with frustration as she waited for the dust to settle, then she smoothed the floor with her fanned tail.

"Dad, why do people get so mad about our decorations? Should we take them down?" Larry asked.

"Son, they just don't understand, but that is why it is my job to teach them. Don't worry about it, Larry. I will take care of everything. Now, let's get ready for dinner," Mr. Lobsterman said.

Mrs. Lobsterman had cooked up a batch of sea slug casserole, with a side dish of sea cucumber salad. She brought the dishes to the table, and they sat down to eat.

"Larry, would you like to say the blessing tonight?" she asked.

"Okay, Mom," Larry said, proud that he had been chosen to say the blessing.

"God is great, God is good. Let us thank Him for this food. Amen. That doesn't rhyme like it should, Mama. Who made that up?" Larry asked.

"I don't know, dear, and prayers don't have to rhyme anyway. It's what you feel when you say them that counts," Mrs. Lobsterman said. She patted his little head with one of her arms.

Larry picked up a jiggly spoonful of the slug casserole and stared at it rather smugly.

"Larry, stop staring at your dinner, and eat it before it escapes!" his mother scolded.

"Oh, all right, Mom. I just don't like slugs. They are slimy," he said.

"Well, get used to it. That's what we eat around here. It took me all day long to catch those things, so you had better eat up," she warned.

Larry took a bite and swallowed, making a big production of the whole process. He gagged, coughed, puffed out his cheeks, and acted as if the food was trying to come back up as he swallowed. His grand finale was gasping for air after he finally forced the food to stay in his stomach.

"Young man, you heard your mother. Now, please behave at the table, or you'll have to spend the evening with no story time," Mr. Lobsterman said.

"Yes, Sir," Larry muttered. He picked around at his plate until he had eaten enough to be excused from the table.

"Can I go outside and play for a while?" Larry asked.

"Only if your friends are out there," his father answered.

Larry went over to the window and stuck one of his eyes out to peek around. There are benefits to having eyes that can protrude out from one's head like an antenna. He spotted one of his friends.

"Jonah is out there, Dad. Can I go?" Larry asked.

"All right, but stay close to the house, and you better come in when we call you," his father answered.

Larry scuttled out the entrance of their home to meet his friend.

"Hi, Jonah! Want to play a game of tag?" Larry asked.

Jonah hesitated before answering. "I can't. My father said I couldn't hang around with you anymore."

"Why not?" Larry asked.

"It's because your dad is weird. He celebrates Christmas—a human holiday," Jonah said.

"You're not going to be my friend anymore because of Christmas lights?" Larry asked.

Jonah shrugged his shoulders. "I'll get in trouble. I have to go in now. Sorry, Larry."

"Wait, Jonah!" Larry called, but Jonah kept moving and didn't even bother to turn around.

Tears welled up in Larry's eyes. He swam back home, his head hung low.

When he got inside the house, Larry went toward his room, not bothering to acknowledge his parents.

"Larry? Is everything okay?" his mother asked.

Larry didn't answer. He just sauntered into his room and gently shut the door. Mr. and Mrs. Lobsterman looked at one another, concerned.

"Hal, you better go and check on the boy," Mrs. Lobsterman said.

"Yeah, I think you're right," he said.

Mr. Lobsterman knocked on the seashell door of Larry's room. No one answered.

He opened the door and found Larry lying on his bed, his tail curled up as tightly as it could go and he was crying. His little shoulders raised and shook with the sobs and whimpers.

"Larry, what happened? Why are you crying?" Mr. Lobsterman asked.

"J—Jonah. He won't play with me anymore because of our Christmas lights," Larry sobbed.

"Oh, I see. Do you think he was a good friend, in that case?" his dad asked.

"No, but Jonah's dad said he couldn't play with me because my dad is weird," Larry said through his sniffles.

"Do you think I am weird, Larry?" his father asked.

"Sometimes. I think the Christmas lights are weird, since no one else hangs them up," Larry said.

"Well, I happen to know that I am just as normal as everyone else, but the Christmas lights are strange to those who don't know why I hang them. I'll go and talk to Jonah's father, and he will see that I am not all that weird. We'll get all this straightened out so you and Jonah can be friends again," his father said.

"Thanks, Dad," Larry said.

"Now, which book do you want to read from tonight?" his father asked.

"The Adventures of Swamp Boy!" Larry answered.

"Again? We just read it the other day."

"I know, but it's my favorite," Larry said.

"Okay, Swamp Boy it is, then," his father said. He reached over to the book shelf and pulled out the book. He sat beside Larry on the bed and began to read. Larry's mother joined them so she could read the voice of Swamp Boy's mother.

Chapter Two

The next morning, Hal Lobsterman went over to visit Jonah's father as soon as the kids went off to school.

"Bill, I need to talk to you for a minute, if you have time," Mr. Lobsterman said.

"Sure, Hal. What's up?" Bill asked.

"It's about our kids, Bill. Larry was really upset last night. It appears as though Jonah thinks he isn't supposed to play with my son anymore because you don't like my Christmas lights. Is that true?" Hal asked.

"Well...yeah. It's true, Hal. I just think it's weird, and I don't want Jonah getting any goofy ideas. Who celebrates a holiday for someone we don't know anyway?" Bill asked.

"Listen, Bill. You may think I am weird, but my lights are perfectly normal. You just don't understand the holiday, that's all. You have a right to disagree, but can we keep our kids out of it?" Larry asked.

"Hal, I understand where you're coming from, but you're starting to look like a fruitcake, man. It's only going to hurt your kid, and I don't want the other kids making fun of Jonah just because he hangs around with your son. I'm sorry, but until you get your senses back, I'm afraid Jonah will not be seeing Larry. I have a feeling he isn't the only one, either. Sorry, Hal, but I have to get to work. I'll see you some other time," Bill said, as he grabbed his briefcase and swam away.

"It's a shame you feel that way, Bill. I thought we were friends," Hal called after him.

Unfortunately, Bill was right. Larry was having a terrible time at school.

In addition to his friend Jonah not speaking to him, other fish had begun making fun of him.

At recess, several of the children from Larry's class swam in circles around him, calling him names and taunting him. They began chanting, "Weirdo! Weirdo! Larry is a weirdo!"

Larry swam between them and hid under a coral arch with his tail curled up, arms crossed, and head hung.

When the bell rang to signal the end of recess, Larry didn't want to go back inside, but he knew he would just be in more trouble if he didn't.

The taunting didn't stop once he got inside the classroom. The kids kept calling him a weirdo.

Finally, his teacher, Miss Fishbone, instructed the children to stop.

"That's enough, children! Now, what's this all about?" she asked.

"Larry's dad has gone crazy! He believes in Christmas!" Tommy DeTuna said.

"Christmas? Your father believes in Christmas?" the teacher asked Larry.

"Yes," he sheepishly replied.

The teacher laughed, along with the other children.

"Okay, settle down now," Miss Fishbone said, composing herself. "While it is really silly to celebrate such a strange holiday, we should respect Larry as our classmate and not tease him about it. That will be enough of the name calling and jokes."

Larry felt like a lowly little sea slug the rest of the day. No one wanted to sit beside him at lunch, no one chose him to be on their dodge ball team in Physical Education class, and no one offered to walk home with him.

Larry drug his little feet all the way home, with his tail dragging the ground behind him.

"Are you mad at me, Larry?" a voice asked from behind him. Larry turned around to see Jonah, his former best friend.

"I don't know. I don't guess so," Larry responded.

"It's not really my fault. I have to do what my dad tells me to do," Jonah said.

"Even if you know your dad might be wrong?" Larry asked.

"Why doesn't your dad just take down those stupid lights, and the whole thing will be over with?" Jonah asked.

"They aren't stupid! My dad believes in Christmas because he believes in a man called Jesus, and that is why we celebrate," Larry snapped.

"Even though *your* dad could be wrong?" Jonah asked.

"My dad isn't wrong!" Larry answered.

"How do you know? They can't both be right, can they? I'm not trying to be mean, Larry, but somebody has to be wrong, and it looks like your dad is wrong this time. Maybe you should tell him to give up and take the lights down so we can be friends again. I don't like fighting," Jonah said.

"Well, I guess we won't be friends, because neither of us can do anything about what our fathers believe," Larry said. He scuttled off and left Jonah behind. He was tired of fighting.

As Larry approached his home, he couldn't see his house for all the neighbors gathered around it. He crept closer to see what all the commotion was about.

The neighbors were all lined up, marching around in a

circle on their front yard. Some were carrying picket signs, which read, "Turn off the lights!"

Bart Fishmonger, the head of the homeowners' association, was at the front of the line, chanting through a loudspeaker.

"Put an end to the fights, and turn off the lights!" He repeated that sentence over and over amidst cheers from the crowd.

Larry's father stood in the doorway of their home, shaking his head. He spotted Larry and waved him over.

Larry attempted to cross through the picket line, but he was pushed back by the picketers. Each time he tried, they pushed him back.

"No crossing the picket line, buster!" an octopus said as he pushed Larry aside with three of his arms.

"But, I live here!" Larry exclaimed.

That didn't matter to the picketers. They kept circling and chanting. They began chanting louder and louder.

Larry tried to run through the picket line once more, but this time, he was pushed back so hard that he went tumbling backward. He landed on his back and couldn't get up.

"That does it! Now you have messed with the wrong father!" Mr. Lobsterman hollered as he pushed his way through the picket line, sending the octopus and other picketers tumbling themselves.

When he reached Larry, he grabbed a hold of one of Larry's arms and pulled him right-side up.

"Are you okay, Son?" he asked.

"Yeah, but I am scared, Dad," Larry said.

"Don't worry. I'll protect you. Let's get you in the house."

By this time, the crowd was silent as Larry and his father walked by them. Mr. Lobsterman snatched the loudspeaker out of Bart's Fishmonger's fin and walked right through the line of picketers. He instructed Larry to get in the house and to stay in his room with his mother.

Larry scuttled inside and he and his mother hurried over to the window to watch what was going on outside.

Mr. Lobsterman walked back to his front doorway and held the loudspeaker to his mouth to speak.

"All right, folks, you have made yourselves perfectly clear. You want me to take down my lights for a holiday that you do not observe.

"Before I do what you want, you are all going to listen to what I have to say. You have ridiculed me, you have trampled all over my lawn in protest, and now you have gotten violent with my son. Thankfully, he wasn't hurt. That's taking things a little too far in the name of a cause.

"Just as the covenants for this community allow for you to have a protest, they also allow for me to have a chance to defend myself against your accusations and have my side of the story heard by the council. I choose to have that council meeting right here, tomorrow night. That's Christmas Eve for all of you who didn't know.

Until then, I would appreciate it if you would leave my family alone—especially my son," Hal said.

He tossed the loudspeaker so it landed at the tailfin of Bart Fishmonger. As the leader of the group, all eyes were on Bart to see what he was going to do.

Bart reached down and picked up the loudspeaker.

"Very well, Mr. Lobsterman. You'll have your say tomorrow night. But, if the council chooses to decide that your lights have to come down, you must take them down tomorrow night. Please give my apologies to Larry. I admit that things got out of hand. I think we can all use some rest, so I don't have a problem putting this off until tomorrow. Is everyone agreed?" Fishmonger asked.

The homeowners agreed to leave the Lobstermans alone and come back the next night for their council meeting. Mr. Lobsterman agreed to their terms.

Chapter Three

On Christmas Eve, the homeowners began to crowd around the Lobsterman house promptly at seven o'clock.

Mrs. Lobsterman paced the floor of the house out of nervous habit.

"Oh, Hal, what are we going to do?" she asked.

"Calm down, Myrna. It is during times like this that our faith must be strongest. Let's pray about it, okay?" Mr. Lobsterman offered.

Mom, Dad, and Larry joined claws and bowed their heads.

"God, I really need your help right now. I believe in You, and I believe in Your son, Jesus. The problem is that those people out there don't know who he is. I am going to do my best to tell them, but I am going to need Your help.

"Please guide me and help me, Lord. It is in the name of Jesus that we pray. Amen," Mr. Lobsterman prayed.

Suddenly, Mr. Lobsterman had an idea. He ran off to their storage closet and pulled out an old trunk, which had been in their family for a very long time. He lugged it to the front door carried it out with him to meet the crowd.

"Lobsterman! The council is ready to hear your case. Are you ready?" Bart Fishmonger asked.

"Yes!" Mr. Lobsterman replied with confidence.

Bart handed him the loudspeaker and stepped back to stand with the rest of the council members.

"Ladies and gentlemen, I want to thank you for coming tonight. What you are about to hear and see have the ability to change your life, if you are willing to listen. I know you all think I'm completely nuts, and I can't believe I haven't shared this story with you before. I think it is finally time to share it. This is a true family account of an event that took place around two thousand years ago, and it has been passed down in my family from generation to generation," Mr. Lobsterman began.

"We didn't come here for a story, Hal!" Bart interrupted.

"Bart, the story has a great deal to do with my Christmas lights. In fact, it has everything to do with it. Please, just give me a chance," Mr. Lobsterman pleaded.

"Oh, all right. Go ahead, but hurry up. I'm hungry," Bart said, impatiently.

"Good. Now listen, this is important," Mr. Lobsterman began.

"It happened about two thousand years ago. There was a ship on the surface of the sea above our village. A terrible storm came. The winds were so fierce that the waves tossed the ship about. The water swirled about so hard that the current reached all the way down to the sea floor.

"That current picked up a lobster and a blowfish, carried them up to the surface, and spewed them out onto a rock. The waves smashed against the rock again and again, pelting the lobster and fish with a spray of water. The force was too strong for them to dive back into the water.

"The lobster clung to the rock with his claws, covering the fish with his body to protect the fish's delicate skin from the force of the wind.

"The fish, whose head was just barely peeking out from under the lobster's chin, noticed a man walking on the water. He thought he had surely lost his mind. The lobster saw the man, too. They watched as he walked right past them on top of the sea, in the direction of the boat. The water swirled and foamed around his feet, but it didn't touch his skin. Even the hem of his robe was dry.

"The men on the boat recognized the man, and they

called him Jesus. They marveled at his ability to walk on water. One of his friends, whom they called Peter, asked if he could come out onto the water with him.

"Jesus told Peter to come out of the boat, and he did. He walked to Jesus, but when Peter saw the winds raging, he became afraid and began to sink into the water. He cried out for Jesus to save him.

"Jesus reached down to Peter and lifted him out of the water. When they got back into the boat, Jesus told the waters to be still, and told the winds to be calm, and the storm subsided. The men on the boat fell to their knees in worship and called him the Son of God."

The crowd remained silent for several minutes. Mr. Lobsterman wasn't sure how this was going to go, but he put his trust in God to lead him the right way.

"One of my ancestors was that lobster, and that is why we celebrate Christmas. If Jesus hadn't calmed the waters, the lobster and fish would surely have died on that rock," Mr. Lobsterman finished.

"Well, that sure is a nice story, Lobsterman. A real tear-jerker at that, but do you really expect us to believe your silly little excuse to hang your tacky lights?" Mr. Fishmonger said.

"No, I don't expect you to believe *me*," Mr. Lobsterman said, "but I would hate to think that you would deny the words of your own relative."

A unanimous gasp came from the crowd as Mr.

Lobsterman opened the old trunk. He retrieved a large book, which was quite heavy.

"Here," he said, handing the book to Mr. Fishmonger.

"That book contains the official account of this incident, as recorded in the public archives of Fishyville.

"My ancestor, Sal Lobsterman, gave the account. The blowfish, listed as none other than Octavius Fishmonger, just happens to be your ancestor, Bart. He signed as an eyewitness of the account. The document is notarized by Clammy Crabclaw, and is recorded in the public records, folks. I just happen to have the only duplicate copy, which was made of all records in case of a disaster. You can compare it with the records at the town hall," Mr. Lobsterman concluded.

Bart was dumbfounded.

"Wait! He could have faked it! What if he made it all up?" Bart said.

"I believe him," said one council member.

"I believe him, too," said another.

One by one, people from the crowd began to announce that they, too, believed Mr. Lobsterman.

Bart had no choice but to allow the Lobstermans to keep their lights up.

Others in the town, now knowing the story of Jesus, decided that they would also like to celebrate Christmas.

By the end of the evening, the entire city of Fishyville shone as brightly as a star. Even Bart Fishmonger finally let go of his bitterness and put up a little string of lights around his door.

The council declared that the Christmas lights would be left up all year, to serve as a reminder of the past. Nearly everyone in the town promised to pass down the story to their children for generations to come, so that anyone who needed a little faith would know how to get it, from a man called Jesus.

If you would like to read about Jesus walking on water, check out Matthew 14:22-33 in the New Testament of the Holy Bible.

Christmas Sentiments

Chapter One

My invention was perfect! Three years, six months, four days, and nine hours since its inception, I had finally gotten the formula exactly right. The key was having the proper mixture of my special elixir with the correct proportion of the stabilizer. I, Dr. Ferguson Landis—Gus for short—had the key to the Christmas Empire!

Once I received the confirmation of patent from the U.S. Patent Office, I was ready to begin marketing my product. I knew exactly where to start. I packaged the product in a small, black velvet box, with a large, red ribbon wrapped around it, and a red bow on top. I grabbed my top hat and wool coat, and set forth on my journey.

I received quite a few glares and sideways glances, as well as a few snickers. Considering it was dead in the middle of July, I suppose they weren't out of line to think I had gone batty. In retrospect, I suppose I could have waited until I reached my destination before donning my winter apparel, but at least the day was slightly cooler than usual, and the walk was a short one.

Soon, I was sitting just outside the president's office at the largest candy company within three states. Cupperton's Confections had been making their candies for years. The company was famous for their Whirlygiggles, which were hard candies shaped like little tops that children could play with, then unwrap and eat.

Mr. Cupperton had become a very wealthy man from the sale of Whirlygiggles alone. Soon, he would become much richer, as would I.

The receptionist announced my presence to her employer, and I was allowed entry into the huge corner office overlooking the city.

Mr. Cupperton greeted me with a firm handshake and a warm smile.

"What brings you to see me, Mr. Landis?" he asked.

"Only the newest breakthrough in confectionary delight," I responded.

"May I take your coat, Sir?" the receptionist asked, but I insisted that it I leave it on.

With a look of sheer revulsion, she nodded and left us to our business.

Mr. Cupperton looked at me with a perplexed expression.

"Sir, I would like to cut to the chase. I have in this velvet box, the ultimate of all Christmas gifts. This small box will equate to a mountain of cash as it brings delight to many people," I told him, and I saw the interest begin to percolate within his mind.

"Well, let's have a look at it, then," he said.

I handed him the box. He untied the ribbon and opened the soft velvet cover. His hand reached in to grab the small tin inside. He turned it over in his palm, observing all sides, rattling the precious pieces inside.

"Mints?" he asked, "Surely you know we already carry a large line of mints."

"Yes, Sir, but you have never seen any like this. These are no ordinary mints. Please, try one," I offered.

He opened the top, shook out a small, white mint into his hand, and popped it into his mouth. I could tell that the flavor was nothing new to him. He almost seemed bored, until *it* happened.

I knew the exact moment when the chemical reaction took place. His eyes grew wide. He looked around, as if he were staring into some far away land. Then, the laughter and giggles came. A moment later, it had passed, and he looked at me with utter amazement.

"Well, what do you think?" I asked.

"Amazing! Absolutely amazing! I saw a memory from

my childhood. We were at my grandmother's home, decorating the Christmas tree. My grandmother's cat climbed all the way up to the top and turned the whole tree over, spilling the ornaments all over the floor! We all just cackled at the site.

"Why, I haven't thought of that in years! What are these things?" he asked, as he looked back at the tin of mints in his hand.

"Those are my special Christmas mints, which contain an exclusive formula that I developed myself. Once in your mouth, the mint begins to dissolve, mixing the harmless chemicals, which evokes a response from the area inside your brain that stores memories. My formula is designed to help people remember their most treasured Christmas memories and sentiments; hence, the name—Senti-mints. Aren't they remarkable?"

Mr. Cupperton was nearly at a loss for words. Obviously a man who was careful not to blurt out his opinions during a possible business venture, he pulled a scratch pad from his drawer and feverishly jotted some notes. He then drilled me on all of the possible questions and scenarios about my invention. How safe was it? How expensive? Had it been tested thoroughly for long-term effects? What if bad memories ever popped up?

Of course, he received all of the positive answers he was looking for. I assured him that if someone had only bad memories, then nothing would happen at all. That sad individual would just receive the pure enjoyment of a fresh mint. The risk of that disappointment was quite low, indeed. After all, how many people could there possibly be that didn't have a single happy Christmas memory?

A few more questions, answers, and papers later we had a contract! Although the contract was just for one Christmas season's worth of mints, I had gotten a very handsome advance check equaling much more than an old man like me could ever need, especially living alone.

I was sure to include a stipulation in the contract that I could do all of my work from my home. Cupperton's factory would manufacture the mints, and at the end of each week I would drop off my secret potion and the special lining for the tins—the two most important, yet still secret, ingredients. It was the perfect arrangement!

All through the summer and into the fall, Mr. Cupperton worked on the advertising and marketing while I slaved away on the potion and liners. What felt like millions of tins of mints to me was really just a few thousand.

By the time Thanksgiving came, everyone in our state knew about my precious Senti-mints. Cupperton had been on talk shows, radio shows, and magazine covers. The world waited with anticipation for the release of the exciting new invention. Senti-mints would hit the shelves on midnight of Thanksgiving, and sell right through to Christmas Eve.

Chapter Two

Just as I thought, my mints sold like hotcakes! The reviews were astounding! Children loved them, parents loved them, grandparents and great-grandparents loved them, too! For all I know, even some pets may have enjoyed them!

Mr. Cupperton called to congratulate me and asked if we could meet after the holidays to renew our contract. I said that I would certainly think about it. He attempted to further encourage me by sending the bonus check from the outlandish sales. Quite a hefty sum, indeed, but I told him that I would rather discuss a renewal contract after the holidays.

On Christmas Eve, I was thoroughly exhausted. I hadn't even had time to really sit down and enjoy

Christmas, but that was really nothing new. I decided that it was time for me to finally enjoy the holiday.

I grabbed the lone remainder of the tins from the last batch. I purposefully had held one tin out for myself. I sat on the frumpy old leather couch and popped one of the tiny peppermint squares into my mouth. The mint flavor really was quite excellent. It dissolved in a rather velvety manner, slowly melting away on my tongue. As usual, there were no memories for me. It was worth a try, I supposed.

You see, I had only had bad memories of Christmas growing up. I was orphaned when I was just an infant, and was sent to be raised by a bitter old aunt who only took me in so she would have extra help around the farm. We were quite poor, eating cornmeal mush for two meals a day if we were lucky.

She made it none too clear that I was just another mouth to feed and would be another burden for her. I never received any affection from her, not even a small hug.

Christmas was an insult to my aunt, in her opinion. I asked her one year if we could go to church with the other families and sing Christmas carols.

She wouldn't let me. We were too poor to go to church in our rags. If God wanted us to go, then she guessed He would send us some clothes. I don't think the bitter old lady ever asked God, or anybody else for that matter, for clothes.

I think she died of bitterness, and unfortunately, it took me quite a while to learn how to not be bitter myself. I was old, and had never been married. No one wanted me now. I had no family, no one to care for, and no one to care for me.

I just wanted one happy Christmas. Was that too much to ask?

Well, I wasn't going to chance it. I had prepared for this Christmas. If I couldn't have my own memories, then I would share the memories of others—unbeknownst to them, of course!

I got up from the couch, made my way over to the laboratory table, and cleared away some of the leftover trash from all of my recent hard work. Under a tarp in the corner of the table was my true masterpiece.

I pulled off the tarp, revealing the handmade wooden box, with all sorts of wires and gadgetry attached to it. I picked it up, hauled it over to the window and placed it on a small table. I fastened the tall, slender cylinder to the top, hooked the cable up to the back of my television set, and connected the power. It was only a few seconds before I began receiving the pictures.

The box on the table began to light up with blinks and sound off with beeps as it received data from the mint tins.

The liners in the tins had a special transmitter, nearly invisible to the naked eye. When a person ate a mint and experienced a happy Christmas memory, the chemicals of the mints traveled very quickly through the body's system, exiting through the skin, along with the tiny particles of memories. This "waste" reacted with the alloy of the tin while the person held it in their hand. The device inside the tin recorded the memories and held them until I turned on the receiver in my apartment.

Soon, I would see the jolly Christmas memories of everyone who had enjoyed my mints! It would be just like we were spending Christmas together!

I watched as the television began to light up with images and sounds of laughter, joy, and singing. I watched for quite a long time, while scene after scene flashed onto the screen.

Frankly, one can only witness so many toy trains, pellet guns, and dolls being pulled from a delicately wrapped box. After a couple of hours of this, I had really gotten my fill, but at the same time I still felt quite empty inside. I shut off the television and unhooked the receiver.

Chapter Three

As I stood at the window, feeling even more sorry for myself and lonely, I began to feel as though I was smothering from the heat. I seemed to be fine just moments before, but now felt as though I couldn't breathe very well. I desperately needed air. I threw open the window and stuck my head outside to breathe the frigid air into my lungs.

As I continued heaving and gasping, the vapor clouds from my own hot air rising into the sky, I suddenly noticed a small church across the street. I hadn't noticed it before. Perhaps I had, but absentmindedly dismissed it.

The lights were gleaming brightly through the stained glass windows, creating colored reflections on the snow outside. I listened for a few moments. The streets were

ALISSA DUNN

completely silent. All I could hear was the sound of
singing coming from the church. Christmas carols, I
presumed.

I was mesmerized by the sound and wanted to get
closer, to hear it better. As I left the apartment and
trekked across the street in the snow, I wasn't even aware
that I had forgotten my jacket and hat until I had nearly
reached the church. I was still in my ratty old work
clothes as well. I decided I wouldn't go inside. Perhaps I
would just peek in the window for a moment.

I pressed my nose up to an amber-colored section of
glass and peered through to the inside. Oh, how
wonderful it seemed! How happy it sounded in there!
My heart longed to be inside with those delightful
people.

After a moment, I felt a tug at my shirt tail. I turned to
find a small boy standing there, with ruffled hair, and
clothes that were much more tattered than mine. His
shoes had holes in the toes, but at least he had wool socks
on. His big, brown eyes were so friendly.

"Mister, are you going in?" he asked.

"No, I am afraid I look too ratty to go in," I answered,
remembering what my bitter aunt had taught me.

"No, Sir, you don't look too ratty. This is God's house,
and He lets everyone in. I'm going in. Would you like to
sit with me?" he offered.

"I don't know if I should go in. Where are your

parents?" I asked, thinking he may have been dumped off here to beg for food or money.

"My dad is in Heaven. My mom is working inside at the church tonight. We saw you, and she asked me to come outside and invite you in. Please come?" he begged.

His little eyes seemed so sincere, I couldn't resist. I smoothed my wild hair down as best as I could, then I followed the boy inside.

It seemed I had missed the sermon, but there was still time for singing. I joined the boy and his mother on a pew near the back of the sanctuary. His mother greeted me warmly and we exchanged names. Her name was Francis, but I could call her Fran, and her boy was Curtis. I was pleased to meet them.

We sang carols for a while before the preacher invited us to the fellowship hall for a late dinner. I watched as Curtis and his mother went to the serving line, but instead of getting a plate, they went around the back of the table and took positions as servers.

Curtis handed me a heaping plate of hot food, as he did for many others who followed behind me. He and Fran looked as though they really were enjoying the task. They remained at their stations, even after everyone else had been served, to make sure that anyone who wanted second helpings had received their fill.

After every last person had had their second or third helpings, the only food that remained was a single

ALISSA DUNN

sandwich. Curtis divided it down the middle and handed one half to his smiling mother and he ate the other. How could it be that two people, who obviously had so little, could still be so happy and willing to serve others before themselves?

That night, Curtis and his mother shared with me the secret to their happiness. It was their faith in Jesus, and their wishes to try and show others how it feels to be accepted and loved by Him no matter who you are, where you live, or how much money you have.

They accepted the position of being servants for God and sacrificed their own dinners so others could have as much as they wanted. After all, if they had taken a plate, someone else might not have gotten the opportunity to eat with them and meet all these wonderful people. That person needed that opportunity more than Curtis and Fran needed the food.

I realized that the "someone" they referred to had been me. What a lesson of faith.

I felt as though I needed to do something for them for all of their generosity. After leaving the church, I found the stores that were still open and purchased a mountain of items. I called and asked the pastor of the church if he would assist me with a favor first thing Christmas morning. Fortunately, he was delighted to.

On Christmas morning, the pastor and I stood outside Fran and Curtis' run-down apartment. I left bundles of

84

clothes for each of them, toys for Curtis, and enough food to last them a century. We rang the doorbell and hid around the corner so they wouldn't see who had come. I did leave a note on top of the largest box.

It read, "I have waited all my life for a happy Christmas memory. You have given me everything I ever wanted, so I hope some of these things will do the same for you."

We heard Curtis cheer with excitement as Fran cried tears of joy.

I never renewed the contract with Cupperton's Confections for my mints. I didn't need to. Instead, I invented a new kind of candy for children that didn't cause cavities. Needless to say, it was a huge hit, and more successful than Senti-mints ever could have been, and I had more money than I had ever imagined.

I kept going to church, and sat with Curtis and Fran every Sunday. Somehow, over the years, they always managed to get everything they needed. Someone, who shall remain nameless of course, donated a small home to them.

I anonymously donated an updated kitchen for the fellowship hall, and I gladly took my new place—behind the servant's table.

"A new commandment I give unto you, that you love one another, as I have love loved you" - Jesus (John, 13:34)

The Homecoming

Chapter One

Jason barely noticed the presence of the ant as he bit into the chocolate bar. He was starving, and for all he knew, the ant didn't want to live anyway. Eating from the trash had become second nature for Jason. He'd been out on his own since he was 18 years old, now going on 6 years.

Somehow, he had managed to get to a point where he was barely on the good side of the law and homeless. He'd already been through all of the addictions—drugs, alcohol, lustful encounters—and the only place they landed him was in a jobless, homeless world of hurt, where no one loved or cared about him. He had long given up the addictions, but the destruction that was left behind could not be cleaned up so quickly.

As he wandered the streets, checking for jobs, food, and shelter, he spotted an empty park bench and sat down to rest his weary bones. A moment later, an elderly male voice spoke from behind him.

"Young man, do you mind if I sit here a moment?" the elderly man asked.

"No, go ahead. I was about to leave anyway," Jason said as he started to get up.

"No!" an almost thunderous voice came from the old man.

He realized that he had made Jason jump, so he spoke in a more gentle and sincere manner. "Please, stay awhile. I won't bother you, and you look so tired," he said. Jason eased back onto the seat, but decided if the man started getting weird on him, he would just leave. Besides, he was awfully tired.

The old man propped his cane on the side of the bench before making his descent. "Ooh-wee! I sure am stiff today, but praise the Lord, I'm still here."

Jason watched as the man pulled open his jacket so he could reach the inside pocket. He saw the glimmer of a small plastic tube which ran along the length of the zipper and disappeared behind his waist. The man pulled the connecting nosepiece from his pocket, inserted it into his nose, and reached to his side to turn the knob on the small portable oxygen tank strapped to his shoulder. He took a slow, deep breath as the fresh oxygen rushed into his lungs.

"Are you all right?" asked Jason.

After a moment, the old man replied, "I am just wonderful, as long as I remember that God is close by. I just couldn't function without Him."

"Well," Jason muttered, "I guess that explains why He hasn't been anywhere near me when I've needed him. He's always been with you."

"What do you mean?" asked the concerned man.

"I've been living on the streets for three years. I have to scrounge to eat, beg for money, and I have no place to sleep. So, why hasn't God helped me? Where's He been?"

The old man nodded his head and replied, "I see. If I can answer your questions, are you willing to listen? I mean *really* listen, with your heart? Before you answer, just promise to hear me out. It will only take a few minutes. Then, you can take off if you want to."

Jason sighed. He knew that the old man wasn't going to give up. He had already heard all of the same old reasons and excuses before, so what was one more? Besides, he really had nowhere else to go. He figured he could tune out the redundant parts and humor the man. "Yeah, I think I have a few minutes to spare," he remarked.

"Young man, I only hear people ask where God has been during the hard times in their lives. Do they ever stop after getting a paycheck or a good bill of health and ask God where He is? Seems like they couldn't care less where God is until something doesn't go their way.

"Now, before you go getting offended, you promised to listen to everything I had to say," the man reminded Jason.

"Yeah, but why didn't He answer me when I asked Him for food and a place to live? What about all this 'ask and receive' stuff I keep hearing about? Where was He then?"

"Are you hungry now?" the man asked.

Jason, looking defeated, admitted, "Yes, I am. I haven't eaten a full meal in a couple of weeks. I have been scrounging around garbage cans for the last few days, and using whatever change I can find to get a few things here and there."

"Why haven't you asked me? If you asked me right now, I would gladly give you something to eat," the old man offered.

"Pride kept me from asking people for things. Do you really want to give me food?" Jason asked.

"Just ask," the old man answered sincerely.

"Can I please have something to eat?" Jason asked, unsure if the man was playing a cruel joke, or if he was really sincere.

The old man shifted his position on the bench so he could face Jason, then he pulled a small foil-wrapped object from his coat pocket and handed it over. Jason graciously took the bundle and unwrapped it. It was a packet of blueberry Pop-Tarts, his all-time favorite food when he lived at home. It was so simple, but such a sight for sore eyes!

"Thanks! Thank you so much!" Jason began chowing down.

The old man continued talking while Jason ate. "Now, let's get to the point. You listen, and I'll talk. You left home because you turned your back against the values your parents tried to teach you. You were raised in a Christian family, but chose to reject those values and take up the sinful life you have led up until now. You were taught that Jesus died on the cross for your sins, but you never accepted it, and you never put your trust in God in the first place."

Jason stopped eating and stared at the old man. He wasn't offended, but the man had his attention just by being so straightforward.

"After you left home, you continued to live a sinful life, poisoning your body with drugs and alcohol, indulging in lustful and lewd acts, partaking of everything sinful in this world. All the while, preachers, teachers, your parents, loved ones, and friends tried to help you. God was trying to reach you through those people, but you pushed them away, along with God," he said.

The old man spoke with passion, and didn't even seem

to stop to take a breath. "By the way, you never asked God for help. You never gave Him the time of day, except to lash out in anger for not catering to your every selfish desire. You accused Him of not existing, and challenged Him to show you signs of His existence."

Jason was enthralled, and couldn't seem to turn his thoughts away from the message.

"One night, you were lying on the street, and a man stopped to offer you a place to stay at the church, but you refused because you said you didn't want help from a god that didn't exist. You say that no one cares about you, but your mother has been on her knees praying for you every night since the day you left," the old man said.

Jason was fully captured by the man's words. How did he know these personal things? Could it really be that much of a coincidence?

The old man kept talking while he had the chance. "Your parents love you and care about you, and God loves you and cares about you, too. The problem is *you*, Jason, not them. *You* took the drugs, *you* drank the alcohol, *you* chose to live the life of a sinner, and not of a righteous person.

"You never gave God the opportunity to show you His power, grace, and love, because you never opened your heart to Him in the first place. You publicly said you didn't believe in Him. So tell me, Jason, how can you expect help from, or even place blame on, someone you don't even think exists?"

The old man didn't wait for Jason to answer. He reached into his pocket again, retrieved an envelope, and handed it to Jason. Then, he stood up and turned to Jason one last time.

"Jason, I know your name and everything about you because God sent me here to help you. The envelope contains a card with instructions on what to do if you are ready to straighten out your life. It's time for me to go, but I hope you've heard the message this time."

The man turned and sauntered off, leaving Jason sitting there in amazement.

As Jason watched the man leave, he noticed that the oxygen tank seemed to have vanished, and the cane as well. As the man walked farther into the distance, he seemed to vanish into the trees.

Chapter Two

Still in shock from the unusual encounter, Jason looked to see if anyone else was around. The park had darkened now. All of the businesses had closed, and he appeared to be alone.

He opened the envelope that the old man had given him, pulled out the card, and read over it. The message was one he had heard before, but he really couldn't ignore it this time. He felt the need and desire in his heart to make things right in his life.

He was willing now, after being so broken by this world, to finally give in and just trust someone, something. He had known all along that God existed—he just didn't want to believe it. He had selfishly blamed God for all of his own terrible actions, and it was time to grow up and accept responsibility for those actions. He got up, turned around, and knelt to pray the prayer on the card.

"God, I don't know You. I am a sinner, and I denied You and didn't trust in You. I have been taught that Jesus died on the cross for my sins, and I know I don't deserve it. I have made a terrible mess of my life right now, and I can't fix it by myself. I want to change my life, and I want to begin living like I should. I trust You to help me change, and I'm willing to accept You into my heart.

"Please come into my life, God, and help me," Jason wept.

He put the card down and continued to pray on his own. "God, I am so sorry for everything. I'm sorry for leaving my parents on bad terms, and I'm sorry for turning my back on You. I'm sorry for everything I have done that has hurt You or anyone else, or even myself. I don't know what to do, but I just need You to help me. Please forgive me and help me to do better. Help me to get my life back."

As Jason prayed, he felt this sudden warmth in his heart. It was the most amazing feeling he had ever felt. It was a feeling of joy, warmth, and love, all rolled into one. He couldn't help but smile, it consumed him so. He felt the best he had in a very long time.

He sat back on the bench, and grabbed the envelope that the card came in. He began to put the card back inside, but it wouldn't slide back in correctly. Something was stuck in the envelope. He pulled the card back out to see what the problem was, and noticed another small envelope inside with his name written on it. He could have sworn it wasn't in there before. He pulled it out of the larger envelope and gently slid his finger under the flap to open it.

Inside, he found money and a small card with an address on it. His parents' names were also written on it. Under the address was written, "They are waiting. Go home, Jason."

Jason was shocked. He looked around to see if maybe he had fallen asleep and was dreaming. He noticed a taxi-cab parked at the curb. He *knew* it wasn't there a moment ago. It had to be a gift from God. He hailed to the driver, and gave him the address to take him to. The driver didn't hassle him or ask him to prepay as others had, but was actually very nice, and drove where Jason instructed him to go.

As he got out of the taxi, Jason realized that he had been given exactly enough money to pay for the cab fare and a tip. He slowly walked up to the front door of his parents' new house and rang the doorbell. The seconds seemed like hours as he heard someone walk to the door. When it opened, his mother almost looked afraid to see him.

He immediately started talking before she could close

the door. "Mom, please just hear me out. I know I've screwed up, and I know I must look a mess. I have treated you and Dad terribly, and I don't blame you if you turn me away again. I know it will be hard for you to trust me, but I would like to try. I have accepted Jesus into my heart, and everything is going to be okay now. It just happened about an hour ago."

Jason continued before his mother could shut the door. "This man came along about dinner-time today as I was sitting on a park bench, and he told me things about myself that no one else knew. Then, he gave me this card, and he disappeared. I read it and prayed, and it's just so wonderful!" Jason spoke quickly, and smiled the entire time.

Jason's mother took the card and read it.

By this time, his father had come to see what the ruckus was about, so Jason filled him in while his mother read.

She began weeping. "We had just knelt to pray for you right at that moment. It was an angel. It had to be an angel," she looked at Jason before embracing him, "My baby! Oh, my baby has finally come home!"

"Son, I think this is the best Christmas present we have ever gotten," Jason's father tearfully said.

"It's Christmas?" Jason asked.

"Didn't you see all the Christmas lights on our bushes and windows? I know you must have seen Christmas lights and decorations on your way here," his father said.

"Wow! I didn't see them. I guess I was just too caught up in my own self pity and my heart was too hardened to see them before today. On the way here I suppose I was so excited about the good news that I just didn't notice all the lights and decorations," Jason answered. His expression changed when it finally sunk in that it was Christmas. He remembered all the parties his family held for their Sunday school class.

"Oh...it really is Christmas, isn't it? I'm sorry. I forgot this was a busy night for you. If I'm interrupting a Christmas party or something, I can just go back to the city," Jason answered.

"Oh, Jason, we were supposed to go over to the Henderson's tonight, but your father and I felt that we should just have a quiet evening at home. Now I can see that God was truly working a miracle tonight. We needed to be here...for you," his mother answered.

"Your home is here, Jason. As long as you need it to be," his father said.

"I love you both so much, and I can never say I am sorry enough. I just want to make things right again. I want to have a family who loves me, and I want to have good friends again. Can you ever forgive me for what I have done? Can we become a family again?" Jason cried.

"Honey, you have already been forgiven. It doesn't mean that you are perfect now, or that you won't make mistakes, but it only matters now that you are sincere when you ask God for help. We have a lot of work to do, but we can do it together, with God's help," she said.

"Welcome home, Jason. We have missed you so much," his father said, as he reached out to embrace Jason. His mother joined them and hugged tightly.

A gentle snow had begun to fall around them, the white flakes drifting slowly to the ground and clinging to their hair and clothes.

As they embraced, wept, and rejoiced on their front doorstep, all of Heaven rejoiced along with them. Another one of God's children had made it home.

"Be not forgetful to entertain strangers; for thereby some have entertained angels unawares." Hebrews 13:2

Christmas in Shelter 17

Chapter One

Gabrielle awoke to the sound of a crying baby. She peeked through sleepy eyelids to see a young mother holding the screaming child close to her bosom as she rocked back and forth. The mother spoke softly to the baby, trying to provide comfort to the disoriented child. The red-faced baby finally quieted down and drifted off to sleep, but Gabrielle was already awake.

She sat up on her cot and rubbed the sleep from her eyes. Her mother still slept soundly in the cot next to her, and her father slept on the other side of her.

"I'm sorry," the mother of the baby said to Gabrielle. "I'm sorry we woke you. She's not used to all this noise and excitement," she said.

"It's okay. We don't get much sleep around here anyway," Gabrielle answered. She was surprised that her father was asleep. He usually stayed awake to protect their belongings, and when he slept, her mother stayed awake.

"What's her name?" Gabrielle asked.

"Her name is Luna," the woman answered.

"That's a pretty name. My name is Gabrielle. My mother is Marta and my father is Carlos," Gabrielle said.

"My name is Kathryn. My son, Willie, is right there, asleep," she said, and pointed to a cot next to her.

Her son, who was about the same as age Gabrielle, was curled up on the cot with a blanket, clutching a teddy bear to his chest as he slept. He was probably about thirteen, or so. A little old for a teddy bear, perhaps, but Gabrielle would have loved to have something to hold on to, so it didn't seem all that strange to her.

Gabrielle talked for several more minutes to Kathryn. She learned they had lived not too far from each other in Mississippi before the storms came. Kathryn's husband was missing, and she didn't know if he was alive or dead.

"He is an ambulance driver. They said he had to work so he could help others. He told us to leave before the storm hit. We did, but the storm destroyed our house. We had nowhere else to go. We went back to find him, but the place where he works was destroyed, and there was no way to get in touch with him. The police made us leave before we could find him," Kathryn said. She began to weep.

Gabrielle sat next to Kathryn on the cot and wrapped

her arms around her and the baby until Kathryn finally stopped crying.

"I'm sorry," Kathryn said, "I shouldn't be bothering you with all this. I am disturbing your sleep. I just haven't had time to think about things until now. We were staying at a hotel for a couple of months, but they stopped our funding, and I don't have any family I can go to."

"The same thing happened to us, too. My father is trying to find work so we can get another place to live, but we are just doing the best we can. Don't worry. You get used to living here after a few days. Just be careful to keep anything important with you at all times. Someone took my CD player," Gabrielle said.

"I'll remember that. Thanks for talking with me, Gabrielle. I'd like to meet your parents when they wake up. You can go ahead and lie down now. I am good and awake, and I will watch your things while you sleep," Kathryn said.

Gabrielle said goodnight and returned to her cot. She curled up under the musty government-issue blanket and drifted off to sleep.

Gabrielle's family got acquainted with Kathryn and her children over the next few days. They enjoyed talking about how their old neighborhood used to be, but the conversation always turned back to the storms and devastation. Willie was very quiet. He didn't talk much to anyone. Gabrielle was only able to get a couple of words out of him. Most of the time, he just sat on his cot and held his teddy bear.

"His father gave him that teddy bear when he was just a tiny little boy. It's all he has left right now to remind him of his father," Kathryn told Gabrielle.

"I had some teddy bears, too, but we lost them. It's nice that he has something left to hold on to," Gabrielle answered.

Gabrielle's family called her over for their morning prayer. They began each day with a prayer of thanksgiving, and asked for God to help them to find a way out of that shelter. They also prayed for those around them, for loved ones to be found, for hurts to be healed, and for a glimmer of hope for everyone in the shelter.

One day, the ever-silent Willie finally decided to speak.

"You know that isn't going to work, don't you?" Willie asked Gabrielle after she finished praying with her family.

"What isn't going to work? My outfit? I know it isn't all that great, but it's what they gave me when I got here, so I squeeze into it the best I can. Why, do I look fat in these pants?" Gabrielle asked.

"No. Not your stupid pants! Prayer. It doesn't work," he scoffed.

"We believe it does, or we wouldn't do it," Gabrielle answered.

"It's stupid. We prayed, too. We prayed when the storms came, and our house was destroyed. We prayed for my dad to be alive and safe, and he is missing. What good did it do to pray to God when He wasn't listening anyway?" Willie argued.

"Look, I am really sorry that your dad is missing. We pray to God because we believe He is listening. You might not be happy with God right now, and I understand. I have enough faith for both of us right now, and I will keep praying for your father, and you, even if you don't feel like it. That is what Christians are supposed to do. We support each other," she answered.

"Do what you want, but count me out," Willie said.

"Okay, Willie. You don't have to pray if you don't want to, but you are welcome to pray with us any time if you change your mind," Gabrielle said. There was no point in pushing the issue. She could tell he really wasn't ready to listen anyway.

Chapter Two

One morning, as Gabrielle walked toward the showers at the rear of the shelter, she passed by Willie's mother, who was on the telephone.

"Hello? Can you please connect me to the Brighton Ambulance Service? I need to find my husband. What? There is no working number? What about Stan Brighton? He's the owner," Kathryn pleaded with the operator.

"You have nothing for him, either? Where are you located? Do you know where Simpson Street is? Is there a shelter there? Yes, lady, I know you have other callers to talk to, but this is important. This is my husband! I need to find my husband! Hello? Hello?"

Kathryn melted into tears as her call was disconnected. She couldn't understand why no one would help her. She had been calling hospitals and the Red Cross almost every day for about three months now, searching for her husband, Charles. She never felt so hopeless.

Gabrielle went and got her mother and father, and they helped Kathryn to a small, private office off of the main area. The gentleman who worked in the office agreed to let them have a few minutes of privacy.

Kathryn sobbed and sobbed as she clung to Marta and Carlos while Gabrielle held and soothed Luna. When she was finally out of tears, Kathryn let out a sigh. Marta and Carlos let go of her and gave her some room to breathe.

"I guess it just hadn't hit me until now," she said, looking at them with swollen eyes.

"We know," Carlos said, "it hit me after we got settled in here, too. Life will get better, Kathryn. With God's help, all things are possible."

"Yes, it is hard to believe, with all we have been through, but we still have many reasons to praise God each day," Marta said.

"I know. It's just hard to do this without my husband. It's just not knowing whether he is dead, alive, or hurt somewhere. I just need to know, that's all," she said.

"Will you let us pray with you?" Carlos asked.

"Yes, but I don't think I can pray right now. I just don't know what to say, or what to ask for, but I will listen," Kathryn said.

"Fair enough. Let's bow our heads," Carlos said.

"Our Heavenly Father, we thank You for giving us this opportunity to speak with You today. Thank You for allowing us the freedom to talk to You at any time, from any place on Earth. Lord, we lift up Kathryn to You this morning. She has been broken by this world, and we are asking that You help to mend her life, Lord. She is searching for her husband, and we ask that You help us to get the answer she needs, God. We are praying that her husband is safe, but we also trust that if it was his time to be called home, that he abides with You in Heaven. If it is Your will, please help her to get in contact with her husband. Please give Kathryn the strength she needs to carry on during this time of trouble, God. She needs peace, comfort, and especially mercy right now, God. We cry out to You in hope and trust, Lord, as we put this situation in Your hands. Help us to serve You in this situation, God, and show us how to serve others in Your name. It is in the name of Jesus that we pray, AMEN," Carlos prayed.

"Thank you, I appreciate that," Kathryn said.

"Kathryn, I know this is a hard time, but do you have a personal relationship with Jesus?" Marta asked.

"Yes, I do. My husband and I are both Christians, and so is Willie. It is just that right now, I am so tired and beat down that I just couldn't do it on my own. Have you ever felt that way?"

"Yes, I have. You know that God is waiting for you

whenever you are ready to talk. We are also here for you in any way we can be," Marta said. She and Carlos hugged her, and Gabrielle returned Luna to her mother. They left Kathryn to have a few moments alone.

Kathryn felt so much lighter, but still not at peace. She finally realized that there was no better time than now to pray on her own. She sat Luna on the puffy chair beside her, got on the floor, and knelt in front of the chair with her hands clasped together on the edge of the seat.

"God, I don't know what to say, only that I just need You so badly right now. I have never needed You more in my entire life, and I don't know what to do. I don't know who to talk to, and I don't know what is happening to my life right now. I am hurting so deeply, God. I am hurt that my husband is not here, and I need to find him. I am hurt because my home is gone, and I am scared, too. Please, God, take care of my husband and bring him to me safely. Please," she wept.

Chapter Three

"Hey, kid! What are you carrying that stupid teddy bear around for? Are you a baby? Do you want to suck your thumb?" a big, stocky boy with red hair called out to Willie.

"Leave me alone!" Willie hollered, trying to get away from the three boys who surrounded him.

The boy with shaggy brown hair and squinty eyes snatched the bear out of Willie's hands and tossed it to the others. They tossed it in the air to each other, keeping it just out of Willie's reach.

"Hey! Give that back! It belongs to someone else!" Willie shouted.

"I'm not giving it back to you! I'm giving it to Zach," the red headed boy said as he tossed it back to the squinty-eyed kid.

"Hey! Don't forget about me. I like teddy bears, too," said the third boy. Zach threw the bear to him.

"I said to give that back to me, and I am not kidding! Give it back now!" Willie said, more forcefully.

"You want it back? Huh? Do you?" the third boy asked.

"You heard me," Willie said.

"Fine, you can have some of it back," the boy said as he grasped the head of the bear tightly in one hand and pulled the body with the other hand, ripping the bear's head completely off. He tossed the head at Willie's feet and erupted into laughter.

"How's that?" the red headed boy sneered.

Willie's anger welled up inside him to a point he could no longer control. He lunged at the boy who had torn the bear. He swung his fists until he made contact with skin. He screamed and yelled, and kept hitting the boy until they both fell to the ground.

The other two boys tried to pull Willie off of their friend, but Willie turned and began swinging and kicking at them.

Carlos heard the commotion and ran over with some other men to break up the fight.

"Willie! Willie! Stop that," he yelled as he grabbed hold of Willie's arms. The boy was nearly too strong to hold, but he managed to pull him apart from the other boys.

Carlos saw that the boy on the ground had a bloodied nose. The other two had some red spots, but they appeared to otherwise be fine. Willie had a black eye and a bloody lip.

"What's this all about?" Carlos asked Willie.

"Nothing," he muttered.

While one man tended to the boy with the bloody nose, another talked to the two other boys. One of the boys admitted that they were only playing around, and they hadn't meant for it to go so far.

Carlos noticed the severed teddy bear on the floor. He picked it up, and guided Willie to the men's room. He made sure to take him the long way, so they could hopefully avoid running into Kathryn and upsetting her even further.

After Willie washed his mouth out and stopped the bleeding from his lip, Carlos took him to the kitchen and sat him down to talk.

"Willie, what was that about out there?" he asked.

"I said it was nothing!" Willie shouted and started to get up.

Carlos grabbed a hold of Willie's arm and forced him to sit back down.

"Busted lips and bloody noses don't happen over nothing," Carlos said.

"Look, Carlos. You and your family are nice, but you aren't my dad, okay? You can't tell me what to do, and I don't want to sit here and listen to you talk about God," he said.

"You are right, Willie. I am not your father, and you sound like you really don't want to hear about God. But if your father was here, I don't think he would like the way you are acting," Carlos answered.

"How would you know what my father would do? You don't even know him. For all we know, he is dead," Willie spouted.

"Willie, I am not going to try and be a father to you, but I am going to say something to you, and you are going to listen.

"You can be mad all you want, Willie, and you can be upset about your situation. I would be, too, but you are being very selfish right now. All you can think about is how angry you are, and how things aren't going your way. Did you ever stop for a minute to think about how your mother feels right now? She has lost her home, she can't find her husband, and she is stuck in a shelter in a town where she knows no one. She is trying to carry the load all by herself, just for you two kids. Your attitude is not helping her. You are making her life harder when you act this way," Carlos said.

Willie wouldn't look at Carlos. He stared down at the table. Carlos figured he would take this opportunity to talk since the boy was sitting still.

"I know you are scared, and you want to see your

father, but everyone is doing the best they can until things get better. I know you feel as though God has abandoned you, Willie, but trials and heartache are not new. Bad things have been happening for thousands of years.

"You may think God doesn't understand your pain, but he does. Jesus suffered on a cross to pay for sins of other people. He had done nothing wrong, but he took the blame for our mistakes, and he was tortured for it. If he could hold on to that cross for my sake, then I think I can hold on just a little longer through this rough spot until I get to happiness again. No one ever said that being a Christian is easy, Willie. That is why we teach faith in church. It takes practice," Carlos said.

"Are you a preacher?" Willie finally asked.

"No, I am just a cattle rancher. Well, I was, until the storms killed my cattle and destroyed my ranch. The insurance company wouldn't pay us anything, so we are homeless now. I guess God has another idea for my career path," Carlos said, with a little laugh.

Willie was very quiet now, and had gone back to staring at the table.

"Willie, it is going to get better," Carlos said as he patted him on the shoulder.

"I'm scared, Carlos," Willie said, and burst into tears.

Carlos sat with his arm around Willie's shoulders, and they prayed together.

Chapter Four

Christmas Eve was very different than years past for everyone in the shelter. The atmosphere was very somber. Most people kept to themselves, speaking only when necessary.

Gabrielle, Carlos, and Marta gathered together for their morning prayer. This time, they were joined by Kathryn, Willie, and Luna. They held hands and prayed their prayers of thanksgiving and hope.

"I am glad you and Willie could join us for prayer today, Kathryn," Gabrielle said.

"I'm glad you were all so open to letting me in, even when we didn't feel like being Christians. Even though it's only been a couple of weeks since we first prayed together in the private room, I just feel so much lighter. I think and wonder about Charles every day, but somehow I just know that everything is going to be all right," she said.

"You will have your answer in God's time, Kathryn, and we will be there for you when you get it," Marta promised.

Kathryn smiled, and excused herself to go back to the phone bank. She wanted to try and contact her husband again.

"We've got a present for you, Willie," Gabrielle said, as she pulled a brown paper sack out from underneath her cot.

Willie was surprised to have received anything at all, especially after how he had been acting. He accepted the paper bag, and started to tuck it underneath his cot. He felt a little awkward that he hadn't been able to give them anything in return.

"Wait! We want you to open it now," said Gabrielle.

"Okay," he said, bringing the package back up to his lap.

He gently unfolded the crimped edge of the bag and reached in to grasp the gift inside. He was surprised to pull out his teddy bear, complete with its head.

"Wow! You fixed it," he whispered, as he turned the bear over and over in his hands, looking at every angle. It looked brand new.

"I hope you still want him. He isn't perfect, but I tried to sew him up the best I could," Marta said.

"Yes, I want him. I thought he got thrown away. Thanks, Marta!" he hugged her. He also hugged Carlos and Gabrielle.

"I'm sorry we couldn't get anything for you," Willie said.

"Well, I'll tell you what. If you and your family come join us for the Christmas Eve service they are having in the cafeteria tonight, then we'll call it even," Carlos said.

"We'll be glad to," Willie said. "I'll remind my mom."

"It starts at seven. There will be a big dinner, and then a worship service afterward. I think it will do us all good. Don't forget to remind your mother," Carlos said.

Willie walked to the rear of the shelter where the phone bank was located. His mother was waiting on hold for a representative from the Red Cross to answer.

Finally, her call went through.

"This is Kathryn Delmeade. I am looking for my husband, Charles Delmeade. Do you have a record of him?" she asked.

She waited for the Red Cross lady to punch in the name on her keyboard. The seconds of waiting felt like hours. The lady did not find his name in the database.

"Can you please verify that you have our information correct?" she asked. "My name is Kathryn Delmeade— that is K-a-t-h-r-y-n and D-e-l-m-e-a-d-e. I am with our children in Shelter 17," she told the lady.

She hung up the phone shortly thereafter.

"Still nothing on Dad?" Willie asked.

"Not yet, Willie. I promise that we won't give up praying for your father until we know something. For now, let's just try to enjoy this day," she answered.

Willie, who had been watching Luna while his mother was on the phone, handed the baby back to her. He reminded her of the Christmas Eve dinner and worship service that evening.

"Yes, I would like to go. I think it will be nice to feel like we are with some sort of family," Kathryn said.

A bus came to the shelter to take people to a local shopping mall. Kathryn and Willie boarded the bus with Luna, even though they had no money to spend. It was nice to get away for a while and feel...normal. Willie realized that his mother hadn't been out of the shelter very often since their arrival. He certainly had learned to appreciate even the simplest things these days.

When they arrived at the mall, there was a line of people waiting for them when they got off the bus. These people wore coordinated t-shirts and visors, and they were handing out gift cards for shopping.

An elderly man handed Kathryn and Willie each a gift card for fifty dollars, which they could use at any store in the mall.

A year ago, Willie would have blown all of his on toys. This year, toys were the farthest thing from his mind. He purchased a new blanket for his baby sister and a tote bag for his mother, so she could carry her things around easier.

Kathryn bought Willie a new pair of jeans. With the money they had left on their cards, they decided to purchase a gift for Carlos, Marta and Gabrielle.

The store was offering free gift wrap, so they had the gift put in a box with tissue paper and wrapped with shiny, metallic green paper.

The bus dropped them back off at the shelter just before the dinner was about to start. Kathryn and Willie thanked the bus driver and the shelter manager for giving them such a wonderful treat.

When they entered the dining room, it was nearly full, but Carlos and his family had saved their seats for them.

Willie sat across from Gabrielle, and Kathryn sat across from Marta. There was an empty seat across from Carlos. Kathryn filled that seat with their belongings and sat Luna's baby carrier on the table across from Carlos.

"Do you mind if I put Luna here?" Kathryn asked Carlos.

"Not at all. I saved it for a reason," he said.

A woman promptly brought two trays of food over to the table and placed one in front of Kathryn and one in front of Willie.

"We have something we want to tell you," Marta said.

"Wait! We want to give you something before the

service starts," Kathryn said. She retrieved the green package from the chair and handed it to Marta.

"You didn't have to give us anything," Marta said.

"I know, but you have all been so good to us that we really wanted to. Now, hurry and open it before they start the praying," Kathryn said.

Marta looked at Carlos, and he nodded for her to go ahead. She gently peeled back the shimmery paper and opened the white paper box. Inside, wrapped carefully in tissue paper, was a silver picture frame. At the bottom, there was a little plate, engraved with their last name—Sanchez.

"Oh, Kathryn! This is so beautiful, you shouldn't have!" Marta said.

"We really wanted to thank you for all you have done for us. It's for when you get a new house. You can put a family photo in there," Kathryn said.

An announcement from the loudspeaker interrupted their conversation.

"Hello, Folks! We are so glad you can spend Christmas Eve with us. We have a lot of good things planned for tonight. First, let's bow our heads and bless the food," the preacher said.

When the blessing had been given, people began to dig in to the mounds of food on their plates. The server came over with another tray and asked if she could set it where Luna was sitting.

"Well, I suppose I could move my baby," Kathryn said.

"I'm sorry ma'am, but we really just need to squeeze this person in, if we can," the lady said.

Kathryn moved Luna to her lap and stuck the carrier under her seat along with her packages. The server put the tray on the table.

"Thank you," a man said, as he sat down beside Kathryn. "I hope I'm not intruding."

"No, you're not intru—"

"Dad! It's you!" Willie interrupted his mother as he jumped up from his seat and ran over to the man sitting next to Kathryn.

"Oh, Charles! It *is* you!" Kathryn cried. She carefully studied his face for a few seconds just to make sure she wasn't dreaming.

Charles smiled back at his wife and children. He got up from his seat and hugged them all tightly.

"Where were you? I never stopped looking for you," Kathryn said through her tears.

"I was in Shelter 20, just a few miles from here. I called the Red Cross every single day, but they never had heard of anyone named Kathryn Delmeade until this morning. My name had been wiped out of the system by mistake, so that's why you couldn't find me. I discovered that your name had been misspelled all this time. They had you listed as Kathleen Dunleave. When I found out where you were, I hitched a ride all the way here. Thank God I found you," he said, embracing them again.

"Your husband got here about an hour ago, but we wanted to surprise you," Carlos said.

"Thank you, Carlos." Kathryn said.

"Honey, I don't know what we will do now. Our house is gone," Charles said to his wife.

"Charles, I know without a doubt that God will take care of us. If this isn't proof, then I don't know what is. I don't care if we have to live in a tent and eat beans, at least we are together. This is the best Christmas I have ever had," Kathryn cried.

"Me, too," Willie agreed.

They were once more interrupted by the announcer.

"Ladies and gentlemen, we have all been blessed by a special Christmas miracle — the Delmeade family has just been reunited! In light of this blessing, our choir will be singing a different kind of Christmas song to start off our service. Let's all join in for *Amazing Grace*."

Kathryn, Charles, Willie, Gabrielle, Marta and Carlos joined hands and sang it as a family.

Christmas in Shelter 17 is dedicated in memory of those who lost their lives during hurricane Katrina along the Gulf coast in 2005, and in honor of those who made it through in spite of the odds. We watched helplessly through tears when we saw the devastation in your area from afar. You are our brothers and sisters. There were many people praying all across the country for you, and you are still in our prayers. May God restore your spirit and strength as you rebuild your homes and lives.

An important message from the author...

Thank you for taking the time to read this book, and I certainly hope you have been blessed by these stories. I encourage you to read them together as a family. I want to take just a moment more of your time to share some important thoughts with you.

All of the stories in this collection have a special message that God has given to me to pass on to you. Each character is searching for something to make them happy. Everything they try seems to fail, until they realize that what they really needed was available all along. In most cases, it was the need for love, forgiveness, or understanding. I believe that whoever you are, you can find someone to call family. I believe you can find someone to love, and I know that God loves you.

In order to give true love, you must learn to experience it first. True love comes from having a personal relationship with Jesus Christ. When you experience his love, compassion, and forgiveness, you cannot help but share it with others.

Christmas is about the birth of Jesus—nothing else. Some people celebrate that birth by giving gifts, spending time with each other, attending worship services or Christmas plays, or by decorating their homes. However you celebrate this year, be sure to remember *why* you celebrate.

No matter how rich or how poor; which race or social status; which country you are from or which language you speak, Jesus was a gift to all of us. He understands you no matter what you have been through, or who you have become. He understands sadness and suffering more than we realize.

Those of us who have openly received Jesus into our hearts know how joyful it is to accept this gift, and we should share it with others in whatever way we are best able. I strongly urge Christians to use your spiritual gifts so that others may know how to receive the gift of salvation. Perhaps you have the ability to talk to people and encourage them. Perhaps you have money you can spare and would like to help someone in need.

Maybe you have time to offer someone a cup of coffee

or hot cocoa. Maybe someone sitting on a park bench needs to hear the truth. Maybe someone feels lonely and needs a friend. You might just have a coat that you can lend to someone who has forgotten theirs. As for myself, I am praying that someone will read these stories and come to know Jesus as their Savior.

If you have read these stories and you do not have a close relationship with Jesus, or if you haven't put your trust in him at all, I would like to invite you to pray the prayer below if you feel like you are ready to make that choice now. If you don't want to use my words, then feel free to use your own. As long as it comes from the heart, God will understand you. In order to receive forgiveness, salvation, and eternal life, all you have to do is sincerely ask for it in the name of Jesus. It's that simple. I won't promise that everything in your life will instantly be fixed, but your spirit will be.

"Father God in Heaven, I would like to receive the gift of salvation through Your son, Jesus Christ. I want to be close to You. I am putting my trust in You now, God. I want You in my life. I want to feel true love. I am tired of fighting and running, and I am ready to trust You. I accept Jesus as my savior. Please forgive me for my sins, and come into my heart. AMEN."

If you have sincerely prayed this prayer from your heart, I believe you have received the gift of salvation, and I know that you will be blessed. Heaven is rejoicing with you at this moment, and God is beaming. You have finally come home.

"For there is no difference between the Jew and the Greek: for the same Lord over all is rich unto all that call upon him. For whosoever shall call upon the Lord shall be saved." Romans 10:12-13

Rejoice, and go get into a Christian church that teaches straight from the Bible. Grow in the spirit and learn the gospel. Share with others what you have experienced.

For those of you who are still undecided on whether to believe or put your trust in Jesus, I urge you to please visit some Christian churches in your neighborhood. Ask someone there to help you understand the answers to the questions you have. If you are homebound, please look in your local phone book or on the internet. There are many ways to contact a Christian church.

Please don't wait until it is too late. No one knows what tomorrow brings, and I don't want you to miss this opportunity at true love and joy.

May God Bless you in all that you do, and may you glorify God through your daily living. I appreciate you reading my stories, and I wish you all the best that God has to offer in life.

Sincerely,

Alissa Dunn

T. hall

Printed in the United States
63560LVS00002B/1-75